MW00764733

BEHOLD, NO CAVITIES!
A Visit to the Dentist

by Sarah Willson illustrated by Harry Moore

SIMON SPOTLIGHT/NICKELODEON
New York   London   Toronto   Sydney

Based on the TV series *SpongeBob SquarePants*® created by Stephen Hillenburg as seen on Nickelodeon®

 SIMON SPOTLIGHT

An imprint of Simon & Schuster Children's Publishing Division

1230 Avenue of the Americas, New York, New York 10020

© 2007 Viacom International Inc. All rights reserved. NICKELODEON, *SpongeBob SquarePants*,

and all related titles, logos, and characters are registered trademarks of Viacom International Inc. Created by Stephen Hillenburg.

All rights reserved, including the right of reproduction in whole or in part in any form.

SIMON SPOTLIGHT and colophon are registered trademarks of Simon & Schuster, Inc.

Manufactured in the United States of America

1109 LAK

"Today is the day! It's finally here!" said SpongeBob as he bounded out of bed one morning.

"Meow!" said Gary.

"That's right, Gary. It *has* been exactly six months, two hours, and seven minutes since my last dental cleaning. So today I get to go again!"

SpongeBob raced off to brush his teeth extra carefully.

Patrick came to visit while SpongeBob was still brushing.
"SpongeBob! What's wrong? You're foaming at the mouth!" he cried in alarm.

"Ish jusht tooshpashte, shilly," said SpongeBob, spitting out the
toothpaste and showing Patrick his dazzling smile. "I flossed and now
I'm brushing with my favorite toothbrush, just as I do each morning and
night."

"Oh! I always wondered what that thing was," said Patrick, pointing at
SpongeBob's toothbrush.

SpongeBob's mouth dropped open. "You don't floss or brush your teeth, Patrick?"

"Nope."

"Or . . . have semi-annual dental exams?"

"Nuh-uh."

"Have you *ever* been to a dentist?"

"What's a dentist?"

"Patrick, ol' buddy," he said when he had found his voice. "I think you had better come along with me to see my dentist, Dr. Gill, today. I'll call and make an appointment for you."

"Will it be scary?" Patrick asked, clutching onto SpongeBob outside the dentist's office.

SpongeBob smiled. "No, Patrick. Dr. Gill's office is the friendliest place in the world. And what's more, I am their favorite patient. Everyone here knows me! Just watch." He threw open the door.

"Hello! And who are you, young man?" asked the receptionist.
"I thought everyone here knew you," whispered Patrick.
"She must be new," SpongeBob whispered back.

"SpongeBob! You're here!" shrieked a voice.

"Hi, Debbie!" called SpongeBob. "Debbie is Dr. Gill's hygienist," he told Patrick. "She's the person who cleans your teeth."

"Do I hear SpongeBob?" called another voice.

"Hi, Dr. Gill!" said SpongeBob. "Dr. Gill makes sure you don't have any cavities, but if you do he'll fix them."

Just then Debbie and Dr. Gill burst into the waiting room. They joined hands with SpongeBob and sang their favorite song:

"I brush and floss my teeth each day

To ward away that tooth decay!"

"Gee," said Patrick. "I had no idea getting your teeth cleaned could be this fun."

"Oh, Patrick," said SpongeBob, "you haven't seen *anything* yet!" He pulled Patrick into a hallway and pointed. "Behold! The No Cavi-Tree!"

"Wow. Why is it full of teeth that say 'SpongeBob'?" asked Patrick.
"Because you get your name posted up there when you have no cavities at your checkup!" SpongeBob replied. "I get a new tooth every time I come because I have never had a cavity."

"Time for your cleaning, SpongeBob!" called Debbie cheerfully. "First let's take a new X-ray."

Next Debbie cleaned SpongeBob's teeth. Then she polished his teeth with the bubble-gum-flavored tooth polish he chose, rinsed his teeth, and suctioned the water out of his mouth with Mr. Thirsty.

SpongeBob giggled. "That Mr. Thirsty always tickles!"

Then Dr. Gill had a look. "Your teeth look very healthy," he said. "We won't know for sure until we see the X-rays, but you certainly are a model dental patient!"

"Thanks, Dr. Gill," said SpongeBob. "Now it's time for you to look at my friend Patrick's teeth. He's never been to the dentist before."

Patrick got in the chair and opened his mouth. Debbie and Dr. Gill took turns peering in. Dr. Gill buzzed the receptionist. "Cancel the rest of the appointments today," he said. "This will take awhile."

Some hours LATER . . .

Finally Patrick's teeth were clean. "You can each go pick out a brand-new toothbrush now," Debbie said.

"Follow me, Patrick! I can't wait to see what colors they have!" cried SpongeBob.

"Oh, boys," called Dr. Gill. "I just learned that the light box we use to view your X-rays needs a new bulb. Why don't you go home and I'll call you both tomorrow with the results of your X-rays? By then the box will be fixed."

The next morning Patrick burst into SpongeBob's house. "No cavities!" he yelled. "Dr. Gill's receptionist called and told me! I get to have my name on the No Cavi-Tree!"

"Patrick! That's great!" said SpongeBob.
BRIIIING!

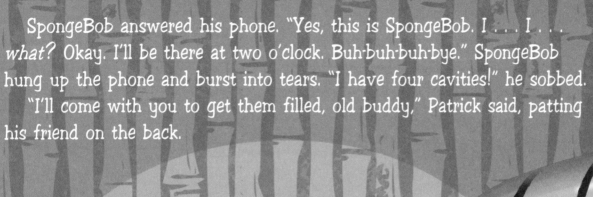

SpongeBob answered his phone. "Yes, this is SpongeBob. I . . . I . . . *what?* Okay. I'll be there at two o'clock. Buh-buh-buh-bye." SpongeBob hung up the phone and burst into tears. "I have four cavities!" he sobbed.

"I'll come with you to get them filled, old buddy," Patrick said, patting his friend on the back.

That afternoon Patrick accompanied his friend to the dentist's office. SpongeBob's eyes welled up with fresh tears as they walked past the No Cavi-Tree.

"Hello again, SpongeBob and Patrick," said Dr. Gill. He looked at SpongeBob's X-rays. "It seems you have . . . wait. These aren't *your* X-rays!"

"They're not?" asked SpongeBob in a small voice.

"No! These are *Patrick's*! My new receptionist must have mixed them up!"

"I have no cavities?" said SpongeBob. "I HAVE NO CAVITIES!" he cried, leaping out of the chair with excitement.

"Woo-hoo! Way to go, SpongeBob!" shouted Patrick joyfully. Everyone linked arms and danced merrily. Suddenly a thought dawned on Patrick and he stopped dancing. "But that means *I* have cavities."

Debbie patted the chair. "Hop up, Patrick," she said kindly. "Dr. Gill will have these filled in a jiffy."

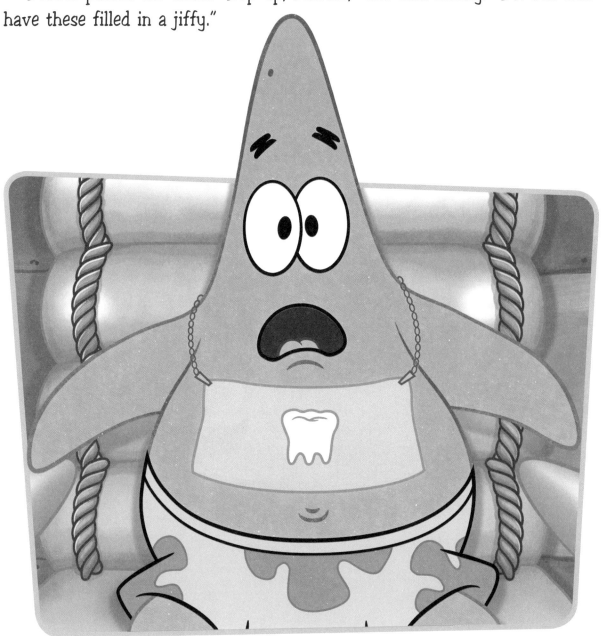

"It didn't hurt a bit!" Patrick said when Dr. Gill had finished.

"Now remember, Patrick," said Dr. Gill. "Floss your teeth every night. Brush them for at least two minutes twice a day. And come back to see me every six months! Now go pick a new toothbrush from the drawer!"

"My teeth feel so clean!" Patrick said to SpongeBob. They watched the receptionist pin another tooth with SpongeBob's name on it on the No Cavi-Tree. "Next time I come I want to see *my* name up on the No Cavi-Tree!" said Patrick.

"I'm sure you will, Patrick," said SpongeBob.

SURF'S UP, SPONGEBOB!

by David Lewman • illustrated by Heather Martinez

SIMON SPOTLIGHT/NICKELODEON
New York   London   Toronto   Sydney

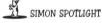

Based on the TV series *SpongeBob SquarePants*® created by Stephen Hillenburg as seen on Nickelodeon®

SIMON SPOTLIGHT

An imprint of Simon & Schuster Children's Publishing Division

1230 Avenue of the Americas, New York, New York 10020

© 2009 Viacom International Inc. All rights reserved. NICKELODEON, *SpongeBob SquarePants*, and all related titles, logos, and characters are registered trademarks of Viacom International Inc. Created by Stephen Hillenburg. All rights reserved, including the right of reproduction in whole or in part in any form.

SIMON SPOTLIGHT and colophon are registered trademarks of Simon & Schuster, Inc.

Manufactured in the United States of America

20 19 18 17 16 15 14 13 12

ISBN-13: 978-1-4169-7869-5

ISBN-10: 1-4169-7869-0

0411 LAK

"HII-EEE-YAH!" SpongeBob yelled as he lunged toward Sandy with a mighty karate strike.

Sandy easily blocked his attack. "Nice try, SpongeBob," she said, chuckling. "I think that's enough karate for today."

SpongeBob nodded. "Same time tomorrow?" he asked eagerly.

Sandy shook her head. "No can do, SpongeBob. I'm going to be grabbing my stick and carving some barrels!"

"Huh?" SpongeBob asked. He had no idea what she just said.

"I'm going surfing!" Sandy explained. "Wanna come?"

SpongeBob hesitated. "Well, I don't know . . ."

"You do know how to surf, don't you?" Sandy asked, taking off her gloves.

"Well . . . sure!" SpongeBob answered, his voice cracking a little.

"Great!" Sandy said. "I'll see you at Goo Lagoon tomorrow then. I hear there are gonna be some epic, heavy, gnarly waves!"

"Uh . . . oh, my favorite kinds," said SpongeBob, not sure what she meant.

As soon as Sandy was gone, SpongeBob cried, "Oh, Gary! What am I going to do? I told Sandy I know how to surf! But I don't know how to surf! This is a disaster!"

Patrick heard SpongeBob's cries and ran over. "Don't worry, SpongeBob!" he said cheerfully. "You may be a hodad, but I'm stoked to help you rip some tubes!"

"Huh?" SpongeBob asked. Patrick was as confusing as Sandy!

"You may be a beginner, but I'm excited to teach you to surf," Patrick explained. "That was surfer talk."

SpongeBob looked surprised. "You know how to surf, Patrick?"

Patrick smiled. "Of course I do! Why do you think I wear these cool surfer shorts all the time?"

"Because they're the only pair you own?"

"Exactly! Let's go!"

At Goo Lagoon, Patrick began SpongeBob's first lesson. "The first thing you do is—"

"STAND BACK!" shouted Larry the Lobster. The big lifeguard set a groaning surfer down on the sand.

"Wh-what happened?" SpongeBob asked anxiously.

"Dude tried to catch a bomb but ended up getting drilled in the zone," Larry replied seriously.

"Huh?" SpongeBob asked.

"He tried to surf a wave that was too big for him," Patrick explained.

Trembling, SpongeBob suggested, "Maybe we should leave."

"Why?" asked Patrick, puzzled. "Are you scared?"

SpongeBob put on a brave face. "No . . . I just don't want to run into Sandy."

Patrick shrugged. "Okay, I can teach you right in your own yard."

Back in SpongeBob's yard, Patrick laid his surfboard on the sand. "Okay, lie down on your stick," he said.

SpongeBob looked around. "But I don't have a stick, Patrick."

"That's what we surfers call our boards," Patrick said.

"Oh, right!" SpongeBob said. He lay down on the surfboard like it was a bed.

"Good!" said Patrick. "Except you're supposed to be on your stomach."

SpongeBob turned over. Next Patrick showed him how to paddle out to a wave, pop up, and stand on the board.

After a while SpongeBob started to get the hang of standing up on the surfboard. "I think I'm getting it, Patrick!" he said, excited. "You're a great teacher!"

Patrick smiled. "Now you just have to try it on a wave."

"Where do we get a wave?" SpongeBob asked.

Patrick thought for a moment. Then he snapped his fingers. "I know! Squidward's bathtub! Come on!"

In Squidward's bathroom Patrick called out directions. "All right! Now try a cutback toward the lip! Catch some air!"

When Squidward came home he was a little upset.

SpongeBob and Patrick spent the rest of the day cleaning up Squidward's flooded house. "I just hope I'm ready to surf with Sandy tomorrow," SpongeBob said.

"Oh, you're ready," Patrick said encouragingly. "Unless the waves are epic. Or gnarly. Or heavy. Or macking. Or—"

"Patrick," SpongeBob interrupted. "Do all those surf words mean huge?"

"Pretty much, yeah," Patrick admitted.

The next morning SpongeBob got to Goo Lagoon early. The waves were GIGANTIC. "Maybe Sandy won't show up," he said hopefully.

Just then Sandy walked up. "Ready to ride, SpongeBob? These waves are bigger than a Texas skyscraper!"

SpongeBob tried to look excited. "You know it, Sandy! I'm stoked!" he said brightly, then added to himself, "I think."

"SURF'S UP!" Sandy shouted as she charged into the water with her surfboard. "Come on, SpongeBob! I can't wait to hang ten!"

"Yes, Sandy, I also want to curl my toes over the front of my board," SpongeBob answered, proud to know what she was talking about. He took a deep breath and was about to follow Sandy when a surfer dragged himself out of the water.

"How is it out there?" SpongeBob asked.

"Awesome," the surfer answered. "And terrifying."

SpongeBob gulped. "Are you going back in?"

The surfer shook his head. "Not happenin', dude. Broke my board."

As the surfer walked sadly away with his broken surfboard, SpongeBob got an idea.

SpongeBob jumped up and down on his surfboard. If I break my board, then I *can't* go surfing! he thought. I'll be saved!

But the surfboard didn't break. "Hmm . . . this stick is tougher than I thought," SpongeBob said, stomping hard.

As he jumped, SpongeBob looked out for cracks on his board. He didn't notice that his board had slipped into the surf, and that he was being carried out toward an enormous wave!

"If I can just jump hard enough, I can break this stupid surfboard!" SpongeBob said. He had no idea that he was riding the biggest wave to ever hit Goo Lagoon!

SpongeBob kicked the surfboard. He tried standing on his hands and pulling at the tip of the board. He punched, smacked, and whacked the board—but nothing worked. This was one tough surfboard!

Finally SpongeBob gave up. "I'll just have to tell Sandy the waves are too big for me," he said, before looking up to see . . .

. . . a huge crowd on the beach—cheering for him! Sandy ran up to SpongeBob. "SpongeBob, that was fantastic! Nobody's ever ridden a wave like that before!"

"Ridden a wave?" SpongeBob asked, confused.

"You rode that humongous wave like a cowboy on a buckin' bronco!" Sandy said, grinning from ear to ear.

"I did?" SpongeBob asked. "I mean . . . yeah, I did!"

"Hooray for SpongeBob!" everyone shouted.
"Hooray for gnarly waves!" SpongeBob shouted back.

NICKELODEON

SPONGEBOB
SQUAREPANTS

WHO BOB WHAT PANTS?

adapted by Emily Sollinger
based on the screenplay by Casey Alexander,
Zeus Cervas, and Steven Banks
illustrated by Stephen Reed

SIMON SPOTLIGHT/NICKELODEON
New York   London   Toronto   Sydney

Based on the TV series *SpongeBob SquarePants*® created by Stephen Hillenburg as seen on Nickelodeon®

SIMON SPOTLIGHT

An imprint of Simon & Schuster Children's Publishing Division

1230 Avenue of the Americas, New York, New York 10020

© 2008 Viacom International Inc. All rights reserved. NICKELODEON, *SpongeBob SquarePants*, and all related titles, logos,

and characters are registered trademarks of Viacom International Inc. Created by Stephen Hillenburg.

All rights reserved, including the right of reproduction in whole or in part in any form.

SIMON SPOTLIGHT and colophon are registered trademarks of Simon & Schuster, Inc.

Manufactured in the United States of America

1109 LAK

"Good morning, Gary!" sang SpongeBob. "Isn't life great?" he asked, picking up Gary and hugging him a *little* too tightly. Gary let out a loud growl.

Later, on his way out, SpongeBob bumped right into his best friend, Patrick!

"Oh, hey, Patrick! How goes it?" SpongeBob asked.

"Great, until you showed up," muttered Patrick. "That *was* a cake for my mom's birthday," he continued, pointing to his chocolate-covered belly. "Thanks a lot. Now please just go away!"

SpongeBob frowned and walked away. Next he visited his good friend Squidward. But Squidward just slammed the door in SpongeBob's face! SpongeBob felt even worse than he had before.

SLAM!

He knew Sandy would be happy to see him. But as he walked into her treedome, he tripped and splashed the water from his helmet all over her brand-new robot. Sandy's face turned red with anger.

"Just GO!" she snarled.

There was only one hope left—the Krusty Krab! But as he entered the kitchen, SpongeBob slipped, slid across the floor, and knocked Mr. Krabs and his crisp dollar bills right into the fryer!

"If I were you, lad, I'd get as far away from me as possible!" Mr. Krabs barked.

Miserable, SpongeBob decided it was time to leave Bikini Bottom forever. "Good-bye, Bikini Bottom," SpongeBob called out. "Good-bye, life as I know it . . ."

After miles of walking, SpongeBob found himself in an unfamiliar place. There were new sounds and scary creatures. It was dark, and suddenly SpongeBob heard a loud noise! Afraid, he ran away as fast as he could. As he ran, SpongeBob tripped on a rock and tumbled down a tall cliff, bumping his head hard on the way down!

Meanwhile, back in Bikini Bottom, Patrick was knocking on SpongeBob's door when Sandy appeared.

"Patrick, where's SpongeBob?" she asked.

"I don't know. I've been knocking on his door for three hours."

Worried, she gave the door a quick karate chop. *Boom!* The door came crashing down. Inside, an oversized Gary let out a "meow."

"Oh, boy!" cried Sandy. "Gary said SpongeBob left a note."

"He's gone! I shouldn't have yelled at SpongeBob," Sandy lamented. "I must have made him feel really bad."

"Me too," said Patrick.

"We have to find him!" said Sandy. "Come on! Let's start searchin'!"

Sandy and Patrick checked the Krusty Krab. SpongeBob wasn't there, but there *were* a lot of hungry customers who wanted their Krabby Patties. Mr. Krabs was really worried! He knew that the Krusty Krab couldn't survive without SpongeBob!

"I'm nothing without my number-one fry cook!" said Mr. Krabs. "Squidward, I am ordering you to find him. If you don't, you'll be out of a job forever! If you do find him, this jewel-encrusted egg will be yours to keep!"

"A jewel-encrusted egg?" asked Squidward, looking longingly at the egg. "My collection will finally be complete! I am on my way, sir."

Back in the unfamiliar seas, SpongeBob finally opened his eyes and rubbed the large bump on his head. Then he noticed two fish kneeling down, looking at a pile of square pants. He went over to say hello.

"Oh, hello! We were just admiring your clothes!" the fish told him. "These are your brown pants, aren't they?" the fish asked, showing him a pile of brown pants.

"I can't remember. I don't even know my name," said SpongeBob. "All I know is that I hit my head and woke up here."

"That's too bad. Let's call you Cheesehead BrownPants."

Just then SpongeBob felt something in his pockets. "Hey, what's this?" he said, pulling out a bottle of bubbles and a blowing wand.

"Not bubbles!" shouted his new friends. Then they ran away!

SpongeBob started walking. Soon he found himself in New Kelp City.

Grrr! His stomach began to growl loudly. He needed food, but he didn't have a penny in his pockets! There was only one thing to do—get a job.

But his fantastic bubble-blowing skills made every employer run away in fear.

I don't understand, thought SpongeBob. Is something wrong with this place, or is it me?

SpongeBob began walking around
the city aimlessly. To cheer himself
up, he took out his trusty bubbles
and began to blow. "Bubbles will
steady the old nerves," he said
to himself. *Bloop!* "Feeling better
already!"

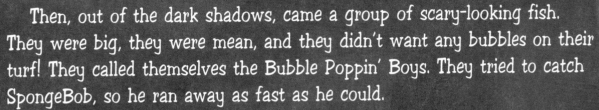

Then, out of the dark shadows, came a group of scary-looking fish. They were big, they were mean, and they didn't want any bubbles on their turf! They called themselves the Bubble Poppin' Boys. They tried to catch SpongeBob, so he ran away as fast as he could.

Then SpongeBob had an idea! He blew the biggest bubble ever—and caught the Bubble Poppin' Boys inside! It floated far, far away with them inside, never to return.

Citizens of New Kelp City flooded the streets with bubbles in celebration! "Thank you, Cheesehead BrownPants!" the mayor said to SpongeBob. "You have restored bubble blowing to the streets! I appoint you the new mayor!"

New Kelp Times

Cheesehead Named Mayor of New Kelp!

Meanwhile . . . Sandy, Squidward, and Patrick continued their search. "There he is!" exclaimed Sandy. "On the cover of that newspaper! He's mayor of New Kelp City? We've got to get there, quick!"

When Sandy, Patrick, and Squidward got there, they were shocked by what they saw—and heard.

"Citizens of New Kelp City," announced SpongeBob over a microphone. "I'm not exactly sure what a 'mayor' is. But, as long as I am wearing this hat, it will always be safe to blow bubbles in New Kelp City, or my name isn't . . . CheeseHead BrownPants."

"CheeseHead BrownPants?" said Sandy.

"Who are you?" asked SpongeBob.

"We're your best friends!" said Patrick.

"Sorry. All I remember is hitting my head, blowing some bubbles, and now, poof! I'm mayor!"

"You must have lost your memory when you hit your head," said Sandy. "Come back to Bikini Bottom with us. We're all real sorry we yelled at you, buddy."

"I'm sorry," replied SpongeBob. "I can't leave. I'm late for a very important meeting." With that SpongeBob hopped in the mayor's limousine, which was waiting for him.

Good thing Squidward was in the driver's seat! "Don't just stand there," he called to Sandy and Patrick. "Get in!"

And off they rode, back to Bikini Bottom.

"Start fryin' up them Patties!" yelled Mr. Krabs cheerfully when he saw SpongeBob come through the door.

"I was a fry cook before?" asked SpongeBob, unimpressed.

"Yes, lad! The best in the business!" replied Mr. Krabs proudly.

"Well, I'm going back to my modest job as mayor," SpongeBob announced, dropping the spatula on the floor. "New Kelp City needs me."

"Mr. Krabs," cried Squidward with delight. "I brought back the number-one fry cook. You've got to pay up!"

"All right. A deal is a deal," said Mr. Krabs grumpily, handing the golden egg over to Squidward.

As Squidward walked toward the door staring at his prized possession, he tripped on the spatula SpongeBob had dropped. His precious egg went soaring through the air and hit SpongeBob—*smack*—on the top of his head!

"You okay, SpongeBob?" asked Sandy.

"Just a bit of a headache, Sandy," answered SpongeBob. "Well, time to get to work!"

Patrick, Sandy, and Mr. Krabs all jumped with excitement. They were thrilled to have him back!

Everyone was so happy that SpongeBob was back home!

"Order up!" he called cheerily from behind the window of the Krusty Krab kitchen.

Things were finally back to normal in Bikini Bottom!

ATLANTIS SQUAREPANTIS

adapted by Erica Pass

based on the teleplay by Dani Michaeli and Steven Banks

illustrated by The Artifact Group

SIMON SPOTLIGHT/NICKELODEON

New York   London   Toronto   Sydney

Based on the TV series *SpongeBob SquarePants*® created by Stephen Hillenburg as seen on Nickelodeon®

SIMON SPOTLIGHT

An imprint of Simon & Schuster Children's Publishing Division

1230 Avenue of the Americas, New York, New York 10020

© 2007 Viacom International Inc. All rights reserved. NICKELODEON, *SpongeBob SquarePants*, and all related titles, logos, and characters are registered trademarks of Viacom International Inc. Created by Stephen Hillenburg.

All rights reserved, including the right of reproduction in whole or in part in any form.

SIMON SPOTLIGHT and colophon are registered trademarks of Simon & Schuster, Inc.

Manufactured in the United States of America

It was a perfect day for blowing bubbles. SpongeBob blew a bubble large and floaty enough to carry him and Patrick high above Bikini Bottom.

"This bubble will break all records," said SpongeBob. But he didn't realize how far they had gone until much later.

The two began to pound on the bubble. "We're never going to get out of here!" they cried.

The bubble finally coasted down and into a cave, coming to rest against something sharp. It burst, and Patrick and SpongeBob fell to the ground.

"What happened?" asked Patrick.

"*That's* what happened!" said SpongeBob, pointing at a jagged piece of metal. He got closer and saw that it said "Antis."

"What do you think that means, Pat?"

"Hmm," said Patrick. "Antis . . . antis . . . SquarePantis! It probably belonged to your ancestors! You must wear the ancient crest of your ancestors, for it is your birthright!"

And Patrick stuck the amulet in SpongeBob's head!

SpongeBob and Patrick decided to take it to the Bikini Bottom Museum, where they bumped into Squidward.

"Would you two watch where you're—," Squidward started to yell. Then he saw what SpongeBob had in his hand. "What are you doing with the amulet of Atlantis?" he asked. He thought they were trying to steal it from the museum!

But then Squidward realized that SpongeBob and Patrick had in fact found the missing half of the Atlantian amulet!

"What's an Atlantian omelet?" asked SpongeBob.

"Amulet!" yelled Squidward. "Not omelet! It's the key to untold riches!"

At that moment Mr. Krabs showed up. "Did someone say 'untold riches'?"

Squidward told them about the lost city of Atlantis. "For reasons unknown, the great city disappeared one day, and no ruins were ever found. All the inventions you take for granted were given to us by the Atlantians."

As Squidward spoke, SpongeBob found himself staring at a bubble shown on a mural. He pointed it out to Patrick.

"That's the oldest living bubble," said Squidward. "It lives in Atlantis."

"It's the most beautiful bubble I've ever seen," said Patrick.

Just then Sandy showed up. "What's all the hubbub, boys?" she asked.

"These two chowderbrains found the missing half of the amulet of Atlantis," said Squidward.

"Well, let's hitch them two doggies up!" said Sandy.

The group watched as Squidward carefully placed the two pieces together—and they glowed!

Suddenly there was a bright beam of light and lots of rumbling—and a huge van appeared, crashing through the ceiling of the museum! The amulet began to spin. It rose up and landed in a slot on the front of the van. The doors opened up.

"Welcome aboard the sea ship *Atlantis*," a computerized voice said. "This is a nonstop trip, so please take a seat, relax, and we'll be on our way."

The gang coasted deep through the water until finally they could see Atlantis below. Then they hurtled toward the city and hit the ground, skidding to a stop. They emerged from the van and approached a long staircase. At the bottom was a bell.

"Go on, SpongeBob," said Mr. Krabs. "Ring the bell."

SpongeBob rang the bell and everyone waited nervously as a red carpet rolled down the stairs.

"Welcome to Atlantis," a voice announced. "I've been expecting you."

With that, someone tumbled down the stairs, arriving at SpongeBob's feet. "Allow me to introduce myself," he said. "I am the Lord Royal Highness. But my friends call me LRH."

"My friends call me SpongeBob," said SpongeBob. "I'm here to see the oldest bubble."

Meanwhile Plankton had snuck aboard the bus after he overheard the group talking about the collection of weapons in Atlantis.

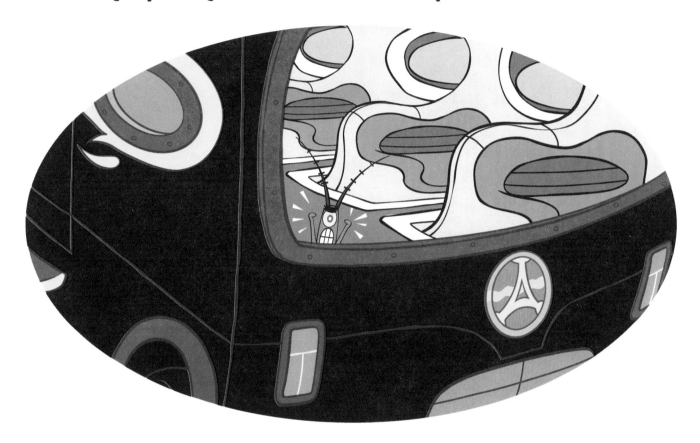

LRH happily showed SpongeBob and his friends around the city. "For centuries, we Atlantians spent our talents and energy building weapons to defend ourselves," he said. "But we gave up the idea of warfare long ago, and now these weapons gather dust behind these locked doors—to show what must be done if one wishes to live in harmony with all creatures of this or any world."

Next they came upon a room filled with treasure.

"Long ago we decided to focus on gathering knowledge instead of wealth," said LRH. The group followed him away from the riches, except for Mr. Krabs.

Sandy was looking forward to seeing some Atlantian inventions.
"Of course," LRH said. "I give you the Atlantian Hall of Science!"
"Hoppin' acorns!" said Sandy when she saw the room filled with
machines. One machine even took objects and turned them into ice cream!
Sandy decided to stay behind in the Hall of Science.

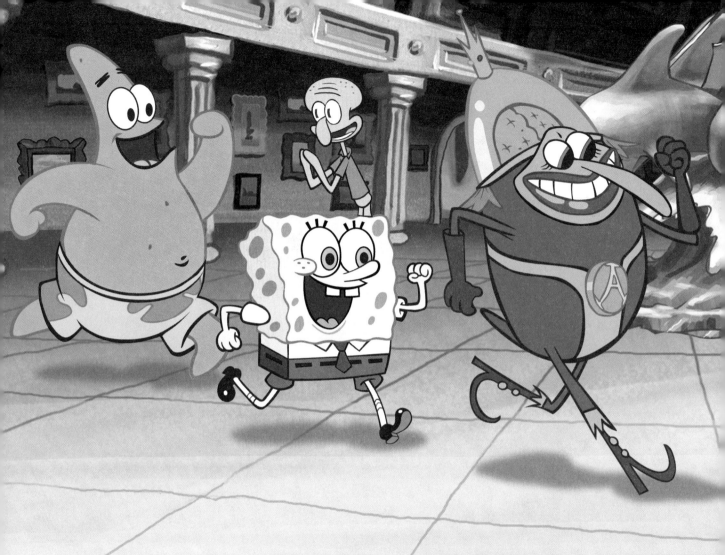

At the Hall of Arts, Squidward couldn't believe his eyes. "The creativity!
The artistry!" he cried out. "Looks like I'll be here inspiring these Atlantian
art makers with my beauty. You guys go on ahead!"

"Excuse me, sir," SpongeBob said to LRH. "Can we see the bubble now?"

"Of course you can!" said LRH. "But first, please remember the bubble is
more than one million years old."

SpongeBob and Patrick ran toward the bubble, which was held within a large glass ball.

"So ancient, so floaty," said SpongeBob admiringly. "It's the most beautiful, wrinkled-up, dusty old bubble I've ever seen."

"Like a delicate air raisin!" said Patrick.

LRH had to get ready for dinner. "I'm going to leave you two friendly strangers alone with our most beloved, ancient, and fragile Atlantian relic," he said as he walked away.

In their excitement, SpongeBob and Patrick pushed against the glass ball and set it loose. They struggled under its weight, finally setting it straight. And the bubble had not burst!

"That was a close one, buddy," said SpongeBob. "We should go before something else happens."

"Let's get a picture for our scrapbooks before we leave," said Patrick. "Great idea, Pat!" SpongeBob agreed.

But it turned out to be anything *but* a great idea when the flash from the camera made the bubble burst!

SpongeBob and Patrick were panicking when they arrived for dinner. "We have to go back to Bikini Bottom now," they said.

"Why would you want to leave a paradise like this?" Squidward asked.

"Because," said SpongeBob, stalling, "I miss Gary . . . and—"

"We destroyed your most prized possession!" Patrick blurted out.

SpongeBob and Patrick were ready for LRH to start yelling at them.

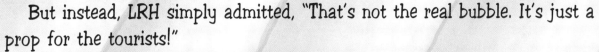

But instead, LRH simply admitted, "That's not the real bubble. It's just a prop for the tourists!"

He took out a small jar with a wrinkled bubble floating inside. "This is the real deal," he said proudly.

"Ooohh," said SpongeBob and Patrick, relieved and thrilled at the same time. Then Patrick took another picture—and the bubble burst!

This time LRH was furious. "Summon the royal guard!" he roared. "Seize the hostile bubble poppers!"

"Let's hightail it out of here!" called Sandy.

With the guards chasing them, the Bikini Bottom gang ran—until they crashed into a large tank.

Suddenly a voice from inside the machine announced, "I am in control of the most powerful weapon in Atlantis! Now bow before the new king of Atlantis, and prepare to taste my wrath!"

It was Plankton! He hopped on a button and . . . SPLURT! Ice cream oozed onto everyone below.

"Mmm . . . thanks, Plankton!" Patrick said between mouthfuls of ice cream. Plankton jumped out of the machine and kicked it, muttering to himself.

LRH was delighted. "Look, a talking speck!" he said. "It will make a fantastic replacement for our recently deflated national treasure."

As Plankton ranted and raved in a jar, LRH said good-bye to the visitors from Bikini Bottom. He seemed very eager to see them leave.

"So nice to meet you all," said LRH. "I hope you have a safe journey home. Do come back anytime."

![SpongeBob SquarePants](Nickelodeon SpongeBob SquarePants)

VOTE for SPONGEBOB

by Erica Pass
illustrated by Harry Moore

SIMON SPOTLIGHT/NICKELODEON
New York   London   Toronto   Sydney

Based on the TV series *SpongeBob SquarePants*® created by Stephen Hillenburg as seen on Nickelodeon®

SIMON SPOTLIGHT

An imprint of Simon & Schuster Children's Publishing Division

1230 Avenue of the Americas, New York, New York 10020

© 2008 Viacom International Inc. All rights reserved. NICKELODEON, *SpongeBob SquarePants*, and all related titles, logos, and characters are registered trademarks of Viacom International Inc. Created by Stephen Hillenburg.

All rights reserved, including the right of reproduction in whole or in part in any form.

SIMON SPOTLIGHT and colophon are registered trademarks of Simon & Schuster, Inc.

Manufactured in the United States of America

1109 LAK

It was a day like any other at the Krusty Krab. SpongeBob was frying. Squidward was grumbling. And Mr. Krabs was counting his money.

"Barnacles!" he said. "We've come up short again! I need me a moneymaking plan, and I need one quick."

Mr. Krabs decided to look around the restaurant for ideas. First he went up to a well-dressed lady. "Enjoying your Kelp Patty, ma'am?" he asked.

"It's fine, but—," the lady started to say.

But Mr. Krabs wasn't listening. "Wonderful! Come again!" he said, as he scooted over to a woman with a little boy. The boy had a crown on his head.

"Say, sonny," said Mr. Krabs, "that's quite a crown you have there."

"I'm a king," the boy declared.

"He wears the crown everywhere," added the boy's mother. "People always ask about it."

"They do?" asked Mr. Krabs.

"Oh, sure," the woman answered. "People love royalty—you know, kings, queens, princesses, all that stuff."

"Is that so?" said Mr. Krabs. An idea was starting to brew in his mind.

"Customers will flock to the Krusty Krab when they see what I have in store for them," said Mr. Krabs, as he walked away. "We're going to have ourselves a royal election!"

Mr. Krabs called SpongeBob and Squidward together. "Boys, it has come to my attention that we need some pizzazz around here," he announced.

"Pizzazz?" asked SpongeBob. "Is that a new ingredient?"

"Hush, SpongeBob," said Mr. Krabs. "We need excitement. We need zest. We also need cash. So I have a brilliant idea: We need . . . a Royal Krabby."

"Ooohh," said SpongeBob, although he wasn't sure what that meant.

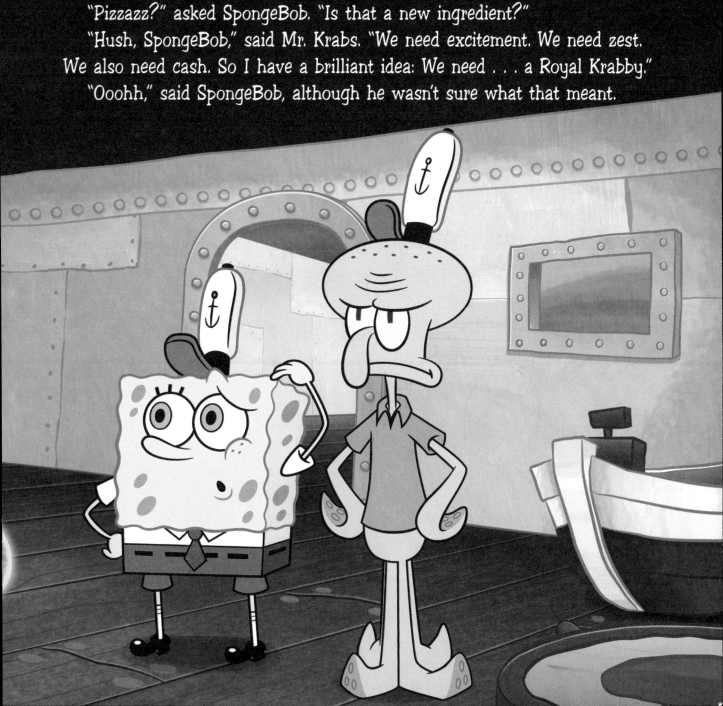

"The Krusty Krab is going to have an election," Mr. Krabs explained. "And the two of you have been chosen to run for office. The one who gets the most votes will be our very first Royal Krabby!"

"Ooohh," SpongeBob repeated.

"This is your best idea yet, Mr. Krabs," said Squidward, not excited at all.
"Look, I've already made your very first election poster!" said Mr. Krabs.
"People can vote whenever they come into the Krusty Krab. So snap to it,
boys. Get out there and tell everyone to vote for you!"

"Isn't this exciting, Squidward?" said SpongeBob. "One of us will get to be the very first Royal Krabby! "

"Thrilling," said Squidward.

"I just want you to know that even though things might get heated on the campaign trail, nothing will ever get in the way of our friendship," said SpongeBob. "May the best Krusty Krab employee win!"

SpongeBob couldn't wait to share the news with Patrick.

"Patrick!" said SpongeBob. "I'm running for Royal Krabby!"

"What's a Royal Krabby?" asked Patrick.

"Good thinking, Pat!" said SpongeBob. "We'll need to tell the public about the Royal Krabby. You're the perfect campaign manager. You're hired!"

"Okay, as my campaign manager, you're responsible for getting my name out there," said SpongeBob. "The public should know and love me. We'll need posters. And buttons—lots of buttons, with my face on them. And a parade. Everyone loves a parade!"

"It's true!" said Patrick. "I love a parade!"

SpongeBob and Patrick stayed up all night making buttons, posters, and flyers. They plastered VOTE SPONGEBOB FOR ROYAL KRABBY posters all over Bikini Bottom.

The next day SpongeBob and Patrick arrived at the Krusty Krab, where they covered the walls with posters. They ran past Squidward, covering him, too.

"SpongeBob!" yelled Squidward. "Get these off of me!"

"Sorry, Squidward," said SpongeBob. "I didn't mean to rub my campaign in your face. Patrick, please remove the poster from Squidward."

"Sure thing, boss," said Patrick.

"Ah, son," said Mr. Krabs when he saw SpongeBob. "I've been looking for you."

"Did you want to discuss official election business?" asked SpongeBob.

"No," said Mr. Krabs. "I want to discuss official work business. Mainly that you're supposed to be doing it."

"Oh, Mr. Krabs," said SpongeBob. "I'm too busy campaigning."

And before Mr. Krabs could reply, SpongeBob was already out the door.

SpongeBob and Patrick went door-to-door so they could get more people to vote for SpongeBob.

"What are you selling?" asked one man.

"Oh no, sir," said SpongeBob. "I'm running for Royal Krabby. And I would be grateful if you would go to the Krusty Krab to vote for me."

"Let me give you a hint, sponge," said the man. "You need to make some promises about what you're going to do if you want to be elected. That's how things work." He shut the door.

"Patrick," said SpongeBob, "I need to come up with some promises!"

SpongeBob spent the next week campaigning across town, making promises to everybody:

"As Royal Krabby, I will have all stores open twenty-four hours a day."

"As Royal Krabby, I will babysit your children."

"As Royal Krabby, I will install more stop signs."

He told people whatever he thought they wanted to hear.

Back at the Krusty Krab business was booming, but Mr. Krabs was not happy. Everyone was coming in to vote for Royal Krabby. Yet SpongeBob was still nowhere to be found. He was so busy trying to win the election that he had forgotten about the Krusty Krab itself!

Mr. Krabs needed SpongeBob back. He decided to call him in.

You know, SpongeBob," said Mr. Krabs when SpongeBob arrived, "one of the finest qualities of a Royal Krabby is the love he has for his kingdom, the Krusty Krab. He loves to be in his kingdom as much as possible."

"Yes, Mr. Krabs," said SpongeBob. "But my world has become so much larger now—and my people need me."

"Well, we need you here, too," said Mr. Krabs. "And I have a surprise."

"A surprise?" asked SpongeBob.

"Yes," said Mr. Krabs. "The election is over! I'm going to tally the votes!"

"But Mr. Krabs," said SpongeBob. "I haven't finished campaigning! I still have to have a rally, and a debate with Squidward, and the parade—"

"Sorry," said Mr. Krabs. "It's decision time." He disappeared into his office to count the votes.

A few minutes later Mr. Krabs emerged. "And the winner is . . .

SpongeBob!" he said. "Congratulations! Here's your royal scepter. Now get to work."

"But Mr. Krabs," said SpongeBob, "don't I have special duties?"

"Of course," said Mr. Krabs. "You're responsible for making everyone who steps foot into the kingdom of the Krusty Krab feel welcome. You make sure that the Krabby Patties are edible and that the kingdom is always clean."

"What about all those promises I need to fulfill?" asked SpongeBob.

"You can fulfill them after work," said Mr. Krabs.

"Mr. Krabs, sir," said SpongeBob. "As your first Royal Krabby, I will do you and the people of Bikini Bottom proud. I will not disappoint."

"That's fine," said Mr. Krabs. "You can even have a dish named after you: the Royal Krabby Patty."

"With fried sea onions and extra pickles?" asked SpongeBob.

"Whatever you like," said Mr. Krabs, "as long as I can charge extra."

"Yippee!" said SpongeBob. "I'm going to get to work right now!"

SpongeBob returned to the kitchen. "Royal Krabby here, reporting for duty!"
"Do me a favor," said Mr. Krabs to Squidward. "The next time I say I have
a brilliant idea, tell me to keep my mouth shut."
"With pleasure, sir," said Squidward.

SPONGEBOB, SOCCER STAR!

by David Lewman   illustrated by Stephen Reed

SIMON SPOTLIGHT/NICKELODEON
New York   London   Toronto   Sydney

Stephen Hillenburg

Based on the TV series _SpongeBob SquarePants_® created by Stephen Hillenburg as seen on Nickelodeon®

SIMON SPOTLIGHT

An imprint of Simon & Schuster Children's Publishing Division

1230 Avenue of the Americas, New York, New York 10020

© 2010 Viacom International Inc. All rights reserved. NICKELODEON, _SpongeBob SquarePants_, and all related titles, logos, and characters are registered trademarks of Viacom International Inc. Created by Stephen Hillenburg.

All rights reserved, including the right of reproduction in whole or in part in any form.

SIMON SPOTLIGHT and colophon are registered trademarks of Simon & Schuster, Inc.

For information about special discounts for bulk purchases, please contact Simon & Schuster Special Sales at 1-866-506-1949 or business@simonandschuster.com.

Manufactured in the United States of America, 1210 LAK

10 9 8 7 6 5

ISBN 978-1-4169-9445-9

"Ahoy there, lads!" Mr. Krabs called out. "I have an idea about how we can get everyone to know about the Krusty Krab: by starting a Krusty Krab soccer team! And Squidward here is going to be the team's captain."

Squidward's mouth fell open. "Why me, Mr. Krabs?"

Mr. Krabs chuckled. "Because you have the most legs!"

At the soccer field Squidward waited for players to show up for the tryouts.

"Ah, soccer, the sport of people with real class," Squidward said to himself. He started to bounce the ball on his knees, but dropped it. Still Squidward was unfazed. "Yes, with twice as many feet as the other players, I'll be unstoppable! Now all I need are some teammates . . ."

Just then SpongeBob and Patrick ran onto the field. SpongeBob was calling, "I'm ready! I'm ready! I'm ready!" and Patrick was chanting, "Soccer! Soccer! Soccer!"

Squidward scowled. "What are you two barnacle brains doing here?"

"Trying out for your soccer team, captain!" SpongeBob replied, stopping in front of Squidward, who shook his head.

"Oh, lucky me," Squidward said.

Patrick looked around. "Hey, we're the only ones here! We're sure to get on the team!"

Squidward scowled. He did *not* want SpongeBob and Patrick on his team. "Do you two even know how to play the game?"

When SpongeBob and Patrick both shook their heads no, Squidward smiled. There's no way they'll pass this tryout, he thought.

"Great players have complete control when they kick the soccer ball," Squidward said. "You can bend it like David Barracuda or flick it like Mia Hammerhead, but the point is to put the ball into the goal. And it's not as easy as it—"

"Like this?" asked Patrick, kicking the ball all the way down the field and into the net.

Squidward's jaw dropped. "How did you do that? You haven't even learned how to dribble, or juggle the ball, or—"

"My turn!" SpongeBob yelled as he kicked the ball the length of the field into the other goal. "*Goooooaaaaaallllllll!*"

Squidward snatched up the ball. "Stop kicking goals! You're not ready for that! Look, it's easy to kick goals when no one's playing defense. But you've got to have a move that'll baffle the defenders."

SpongeBob was taking notes. "Baffle . . . defenders," he muttered to himself.

Squidward tossed the ball high in the air. "Watch my dazzling quadruple scissor kick. What do you think the other team will do when they see *this*?"

He flung his feet over his head, trying to kick the ball as it came down, but missed. His legs got tangled up, and he fell on the ground with a *thud!*

"Celebrate?" asked Patrick.

Squidward growled.

SpongeBob raised his hand. "Captain Squidward, don't we need more players for a soccer team?"

"Yes," admitted Squidward, "but I have no idea how to get them."

SpongeBob went to Goo Lagoon to see his friend Larry the Lobster. Larry was great at all kinds of sports like volleyball and weightlifting, so SpongeBob figured he would make a good soccer player.

"Hi, Larry," SpongeBob called. "Want to join a soccer team?"

"Soccer? How do you play it?" asked Larry, lifting a heavy barbell.

"Well," replied SpongeBob, "it's kind of like volleyball, only instead of using your hands, you use your feet. And instead of hitting the ball over the net, you kick it *into* the net."

"Hmm . . . sounds confusing," Larry said. "Count me in!"

SpongeBob got Pearl to be the team's goalie. She was very good at blocking kicks because she filled up most of the goal.

He also asked Sandy to join the team because she was terrific at every sport she ever tried.

"Yeehaw!" she yelled as she made a perfect bicycle kick. "I love this game, SpongeBob!"

Squidward watched SpongeBob practice with his friends. They're acting like SpongeBob is the captain of this team! he thought. I have to get back in charge—but how?

Then he had an idea. He would schedule the team's first game! Once everyone saw his spectacular moves, they would all look up to him!

By the day of the match Squidward had gathered enough players to make a full team.

"Where did you get the other players?" Patrick asked.

"Oh, they're good friends of mine who joined the team out of deep devotion and loyalty to me," Squidward answered.

Then one of the new players shouted, "Hey, what's-your-nose! Remember, you promised to clean our houses for a year!"

Plankton arrived with his Chum Bucket team. "We will destroy you!" he crowed. All of his players looked superfit, and they could do lots of tricks—bouncing the soccer balls off their feet, heads, knees, and backs.

"Gee," SpongeBob said nervously, "they look hard to beat."

But Sandy wasn't scared. "Look," she said, "we can win if we work together as a team! That's the secret to good sports play!"

"Team, team, team, team!" Patrick shouted, pumping a fist in the air.

Sandy was right. By playing as a team SpongeBob and his friends were able to keep up with their Chum Bucket opponents.

"I scored a goal!" SpongeBob shouted happily.

"And I got this neat yellow card!" said Patrick.

"Um, Patrick?" SpongeBob replied. "A yellow card isn't good. It's a warning—"

"No time for explanations!" Patrick said, running off. "Our team needs us!"

With only a few seconds left in the game, the score was tied. And the Chum Bucket team had control of the ball!

Suddenly Sandy was able to steal the ball and pass it through the other player's legs to SpongeBob! He ran down the field toward the goal as fast as he could, dribbling the ball with his feet.

"Shoot it, SpongeBob!" Larry yelled. "Shoot it!"

SpongeBob was about to take his shot. I'll win the game! he thought. I'll be the hero!

But then he spotted Squidward. "I'm open!" Squidward yelled, waving his hands frantically. SpongeBob hesitated. . . .

But then he remembered what Sandy had said about being a team
player. Instead of kicking the ball toward the goal, he passed it to
Squidward.

"*Nooooooo!*" screamed Patrick.

The ball was in the air. Squidward flipped himself upside-down and
aimed all four of his feet at the ball. It was his special quadruple scissor
kick, which he had never done right—not even once!

Squidward's upside-down spinning kick made the Chum Bucket goalie
dizzy, and he lost track of the ball. The ball sped toward the goal, and—
Floomph!—soared into the net!

"*Gooooooaaaaaalllll!*" SpongeBob called. Squidward had won the game for his team!

SpongeBob watched the crowd carry Squidward off on their shoulders.
"That's funny," SpongeBob said as Larry walked up to him.
"What is?" Larry asked.
"I feel even better than if I had scored that goal myself!" SpongeBob said.
Larry shook his head. "I told you this game is confusing."

SpongeBob Goes to the Doctor

by Steven Banks
based on a teleplay written by Paul Tibbitt, Ennio Torresan Jr., and Mr. Lawrence
illustrated by Zina Saunders

SIMON SPOTLIGHT/NICKELODEON
New York   London   Toronto   Sydney

Based on the TV series *SpongeBob SquarePants*® created by Stephen Hillenburg as seen on Nickelodeon®

 SIMON SPOTLIGHT

An imprint of Simon & Schuster Children's Publishing Division

1230 Avenue of the Americas, New York, New York 10020

Copyright © 2005 Viacom International Inc. All rights reserved. NICKELODEON, *SpongeBob SquarePants*,
and all related titles, logos, and characters are registered trademarks of Viacom International Inc. Created by Stephen Hillenburg.
All rights reserved, including the right of reproduction in whole or in part in any form.
SIMON SPOTLIGHT and colophon are registered trademarks of Simon & Schuster, Inc.

Manufactured in the United States of America

20 19 18 17 16 15

ISBN-13: 978-1-4169-0359-8

ISBN-10: 1-4169-0359-3

1210 LAK

SpongeBob woke up one morning feeling terrible. "Oh, Gary, I don't feel like myself," said SpongeBob. "AH-CHOO!" When SpongeBob sneezed, pink bubbles blew out of all his holes.

"Meow," said Gary.

"Don't be silly, Gary," said SpongeBob. "I don't have a cold. I don't get colds, I get the suds."

"Meow," Gary replied.

"No! I can't get the suds!" cried SpongeBob. "Then I'd have to miss work, and I can't miss a day of working at the Krusty Krab!"

"SpongeBob, what's holding up those Krabby Patties?" yelled Mr. Krabs.

"Coming right up, sir," said SpongeBob, sniffling.

Mr. Krabs poked his head through the window. "What's wrong with you, boy? You're paler than a baby sea horse! Do you have the suds?"

"No, sir!" said SpongeBob weakly. "I feel great! AH . . . AH . . . AH-CHOO!"

"SpongeBob, you're too sick to work," said Mr. Krabs. "Go home and get some rest."

"No, Mr. Krabs," said SpongeBob, pleading. "I'm okay! Honest!"

"Nothing personal, lad," said Mr. Krabs. "But I can't have you sneezing all over my food!"

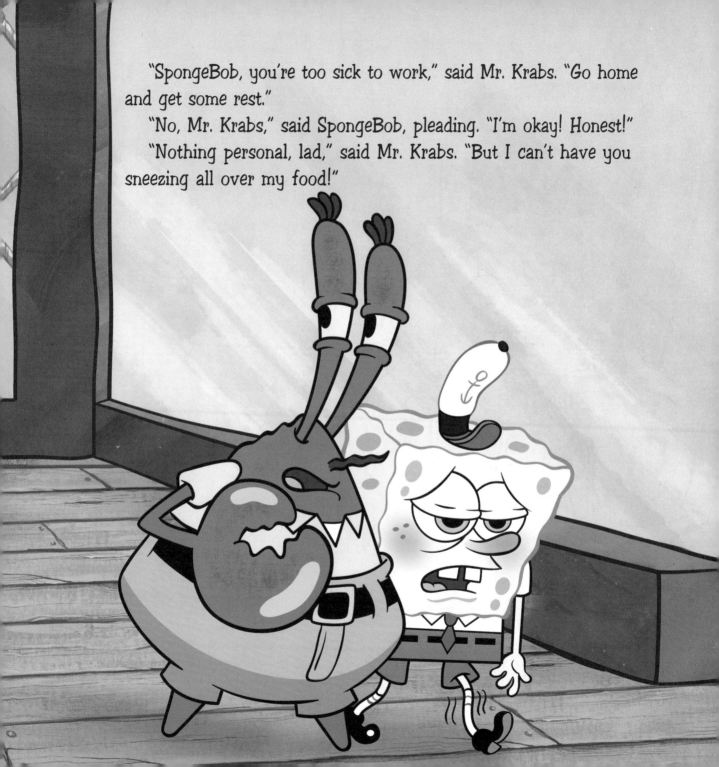

"Who am I kidding, Gary? AH-CHOO! I've got the suds," said SpongeBob sadly. "I'd better go see the doctor before I get worse."

SpongeBob called up his friend Sandy Cheeks. "Sandy, I'm sick. Can you take me to the doctor?"

"Sure, SpongeBob!" said Sandy. "I'll be there faster than you can say 'Sandy, I'm sick. Can you take me to the doctor?'"

"Hey, SpongeBob. Going skiing?" asked Patrick.

"I'm sick, Patrick," said SpongeBob, sniffling. "I'm going to the doctor."

"No!" cried Patrick. "You can't go to the doctor!"

"Why not?" asked SpongeBob.

Patrick pushed SpongeBob back into his house. "I know a guy who knows a guy who went to the doctor's office once. It's a horrible place!"

"The doctor's office can't be as horrible as the . . . AH-CHOO! . . . suds," said SpongeBob.

"Yes, it is," said Patrick. "First they make you sit in the . . . *waiting room!*"

"Is that the horrible part?" asked a nervous SpongeBob.

Patrick shook his head. "No! It gets worse! They make you read . . . *old magazines!*"

"Oh, no!" cried SpongeBob. "I'm scared. I don't want to go to the doctor!"

"You've got to help me get better, Patrick," said SpongeBob. "Will you be my doctor?"

Patrick scratched his head. "Well, I didn't go to doctor school, and I don't know anything about medicine, but sure! I'll do it!" Patrick started putting corks into all of SpongeBob's holes. "There. That ought to do the trick!" he said, clapping his hands.

"Do you feel better now, SpongeBob?" asked Patrick.

"I . . . I . . . AH . . . AH . . . AH-CHOO!" SpongeBob sneezed, and he blew up like a balloon. "No bubbles!" said SpongeBob excitedly. "Doctor Patrick, it looks like your treatment is working!"

"I'll send you my bill in the mail," said Patrick.

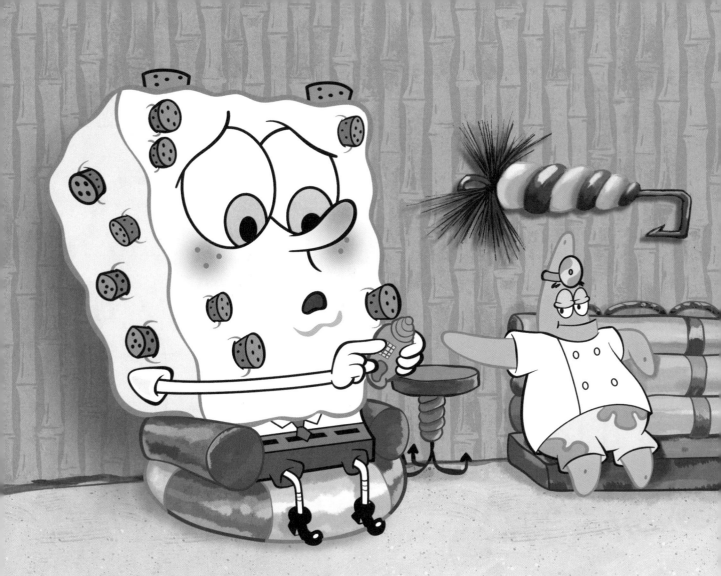

"I'll be cured in no time," said SpongeBob. "I should call Sandy and tell her she doesn't need to take me to the doctor."

SpongeBob tried to push the buttons on the phone, but his fingers were too big and puffy. "Doctor Patrick, will you call Sandy for me?" he asked.

"Hello, Sandy, this is Doctor Patrick. I'm calling on behalf of my patient, Mr. SquarePants. You don't need to take him to the doctor."

"Patrick, you're not a doctor!" said Sandy. "Tell SpongeBob I'll be there faster than a barefoot jackrabbit in a race!"

"Sandy's coming, and she's bringing a jackrabbit!" cried Patrick.
"You've got to make me well or she'll take me to the doctor!" yelled
SpongeBob.

"I know exactly what to do," said Patrick. He put a giant bandage on SpongeBob's nose, spread jellyfish jelly on his feet, and played a song on the accordion. "Do you feel better?" he asked.

"No!" said SpongeBob. "And Sandy's going to be here any second!"

Sandy pounded on SpongeBob's door. "Open up!" she yelled.

"I'm sorry. There's nobody home," called Patrick.

"Where's SpongeBob?" Sandy asked.

"Uh, he's not here at the moment," said Patrick. "Please leave your message after the beep. *Beep!*"

Sandy karate-chopped the door down. "Patrick, I am taking SpongeBob to see a real doctor!" She pushed SpongeBob out the door and rolled him down the road.

"He's fine!" cried Patrick, running after her. "Tell her how fine you are, SpongeBob!"

"I'm . . . AH-CHOO . . . fine!" said SpongeBob.

SpongeBob started rolling down the hill toward the Krusty Krab!
"SpongeBob, stop!" shouted Mr. Krabs. "You can't come back to work!
You're still sick. Plus, there's no way you'll fit into your uniform now!"

SpongeBob rolled up to the front door and sneezed a giant sneeze.

There was no denying it. SpongeBob needed a *real* doctor.

He went to see the best doctor in Bikini Bottom. "Well, Mr. SquarePants, you have the suds," said the doctor. "Are you ready for your treatment?"

"Are you going to make me wait in the waiting room and read old magazines?" asked a worried SpongeBob.

The doctor laughed. "No, silly. I'll give you some medicine, and you'll feel all better!"

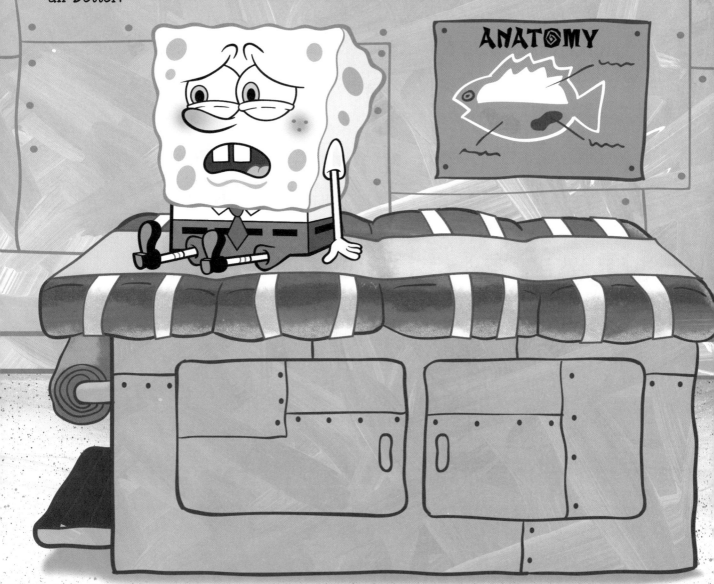

Patrick and Sandy were waiting for SpongeBob in the waiting room.

"SpongeBob, you're all better!" said Sandy. "Aren't you glad you saw the doctor?"

"I sure am!" said SpongeBob. "Hey, Patrick? Are you enjoying that old magazine you're reading?"

Patrick screamed, "Old magazine! NOOOOOOO!" And he ran away as fast as he could!

HOORAY FOR DADS!

by Erica Pass
illustrated by The Artifact Group

SIMON SPOTLIGHT/NICKELODEON
New York   London   Toronto   Sydney

Stephen Hillenburg

Based on the TV series *SpongeBob SquarePants*® created by Stephen Hillenburg as seen on Nickelodeon®

 SIMON SPOTLIGHT

An imprint of Simon & Schuster Children's Publishing Division

1230 Avenue of the Americas, New York, New York 10020

© 2007 Viacom International Inc. All rights reserved. NICKELODEON, *SpongeBob SquarePants*, and all related titles, logos, and characters are registered trademarks of Viacom International Inc. Created by Stephen Hillenburg. All rights reserved, including the right of reproduction in whole or in part in any form.

SIMON SPOTLIGHT and colophon are registered trademarks of Simon & Schuster, Inc.

Manufactured in the United States of America

1109 LAK

"Hey, Gary, guess what?" said SpongeBob one morning. "Today's the annual Dad and Kid Games Day at Mussel Beach."

"Meow?" asked Gary.

"That's right, Gary," said SpongeBob. "It's a whole day for dads and their kids to play games and have fun together. And my dad's coming!"

When SpongeBob got to the beach almost all of Bikini Bottom was already there.

"I'm ready!" said SpongeBob. "Squidward, are you excited?"

"Oh, thrilled to bits," said Squidward.

"Patrick, are you excited?" asked SpongeBob.

"Yes," said Patrick. "I love the beach!"
"Mr. Krabs, are you excited?" SpongeBob asked.
"I'm excited to win the grand prize," said Mr. Krabs.

"Prize?" said SpongeBob. "You mean there's a prize besides the joy of spending the day with our dads?"

"Of course, SpongeBob," said Sandy. "This is a contest. Only one team can win the prize. But the prize is a surprise. No one knows what it is."

"Well, I hope it's a vacation to take me far, far away from here," Squidward said.

"I don't care about the prize," said SpongeBob. "I'm just excited to be with my dad."

Just then they heard *honk-honk!* A bus filled with everyone's dads arrived at the beach.

"Hooray for dads!" SpongeBob called out.

"Dad!" yelled SpongeBob. "It's so good to see you!"

"You, too, son," said SpongeBob's dad.

"Howdy, Sandy!" said Sandy's dad.

"Pappy! You look finer than a jackrabbit at a fancy dress ball," said Sandy.

"Oh, Pearl, isn't this exciting?" asked Mr. Krabs.

"Uh, yeah, sure, Dad," replied Pearl, looking bored. "I'm *so* excited."

"Hello, Squidward," said Squidward's dad. "At least it's not raining."

"Yeah," said Squidward.

"Sheldon," said Plankton's dad. "Isn't this a glorious day?"

Plankton turned red. "It would be more glorious if we won a certain secret recipe," he muttered.

"Patrick," said Patrick's dad. "The beach!"

"I know!" yelled Patrick. "I love the beach!"

"Gather around, everyone," said Kip Kelp, host of the event. "Welcome to our annual Dad and Kid Games Day. It's wonderful to see so many of our fine citizens out here for what's sure to be a great day, filled with teamwork and sportsmanship."

"Yeah, yeah, yeah," said Squidward. "Get to the good stuff."

"There will be many contests all day long," continued Kip, "and at the end we have a very special prize for the team that has won the most events."

"Did you hear that, Pearl?" Mr. Krabs asked his daughter. "That prize is ours."

"Just please don't embarrass me!" said Pearl.

The first competition was a relay race, which Sandy and her dad won.
"I knew I could count on you, Pappy!" said Sandy. "We're on our way to winning that prize!"

"Sandy," said SpongeBob, "there are more important things than winning."

"I think not," said Squidward.

Next was a competition to see which team could blow the most bubbles.
"Ha!" said Mr. Krabs. "My Pearl is an expert bubble-blower!"
Pearl sighed. "If I have to do this, I may as well win," she said.
SpongeBob and his dad blew beautiful bubbles, not caring about how many there were. Patrick and his dad went to look for buried treasure.

Squidward and his dad ended up blowing the most bubbles. "Prize, here I come!" he called out.

"Not so fast, Squid," said Sandy. "You haven't won the grand prize yet."

In the next contest teams had to build sand castles. Squidward hurried to build a really tall tower—but it came crashing down just before time was up.

"See?" Sandy said to Squidward. "You'd better calm down, or else that prize is mine!"

SpongeBob was all set for the jellyfish roundup. "Come on, Dad!" he said. "Jellyfish love me! And I love them!"

In no time SpongeBob and his dad had gathered the most jellyfish.

"Nice work, SpongeBob," said Sandy. "You just might win the grand prize!"

"Really?" asked SpongeBob.

"Still don't care about that prize, SpongeBob?" asked Squidward. "I heard it's something you've been wanting for a while . . ."

"You heard it's a gold-plated spatula?" asked SpongeBob.

"Maybe," said Squidward.

"Oh, Dad," said SpongeBob. "I've been wanting a gold-plated spatula forever! We *have* to win now."

"But SpongeBob," said his dad. "I thought this day was all about spending time with the people you love."

"Right," said SpongeBob. "And I love spatulas. Let's go!"

The next competition was a badminton tournament, and SpongeBob did his best to try to win. He frantically ran circles around his dad, huffing and puffing and tripping in the sand.

"Out of my way!" SpongeBob yelled.

"You know, Son," said SpongeBob's dad, "there are more important things than winning."

"Of course there are," SpongeBob replied. "Like what I can do with that golden spatula! I can already feel it working its fry magic in my hand."

SpongeBob's dad sighed. "Oh, SpongeBob."

There were many more contests, and by the end of the day everyone was tired out—except Patrick and his dad, who had just woken up from a nap. They were in time to hear Kip Kelp announce the winner of the grand prize.

"This has been an inspiring Dad and Kid Games Day," said Kip. "I want to thank you all for coming out to compete. It truly shows the spirit–"

"Come on, already!" yelled Squidward. "Who won?"

"Okay," Kip said. "The winning team is . . . Plankton and his dad!"

Plankton hopped up onto the stage, excited. "What did we win?" he asked. "Is it the secret recipe?"

"No," said Kip, "you've won the honor of having your names inscribed on a plaque that will be placed in a new rock and coral garden in the center of town."

"Uh . . . that's it?" asked Plankton. "I ran around in circles all day long for this?"

Hearing Plankton's words, SpongeBob turned to his dad. "Oh, Dad, I'm sorry," he said. "I lost sight of what it means to be able to spend time with you."

"That's all right, SpongeBob," said his dad. "We all want to win sometimes. But you know what, I had a great time just being with you."

"Yeah, me too, Dad," said SpongeBob.

"Everyone is welcome to come to the Krusty Krab," Mr. Krabs announced.

"For free Krabby Patties?" asked Patrick.

"Never!" said Mr. Krabs. "But everyone can help themselves to as many napkins as they like."

"Woo-hoo!" said SpongeBob. "Dad, who needs a gold-plated spatula when I have you?"